AR 4.8
pts 0.5
162616

DOGS TO THE RESCUE!
MILITARY DOGS

By Sara Green

BELLWETHER MEDIA • MINNEAPOLIS, MN

Jump into the cockpit and take flight with Pilot books. Your journey will take you on high-energy adventures as you learn about all that is wild, weird, fascinating, and fun!

This edition first published in 2014 by Bellwether Media, Inc.

No part of this publication may be reproduced in whole or in part without written permission of the publisher. For information regarding permission, write to Bellwether Media, Inc., Attention: Permissions Department, 5357 Penn Avenue South, Minneapolis, MN 55419.

Library of Congress Cataloging-in-Publication Data

Green, Sara, 1964-
 Military dogs / by Sara Green.
   pages cm. – (Pilot: Dogs to the rescue!)
 Includes bibliographical references and index.
 Summary: "Engaging images accompany information about military dogs. The combination of high-interest subject matter and narrative text is intended for students in grades 3 through 7"–Provided by publisher.
 ISBN 978-1-60014-956-6 (hardcover : alk. paper)
 1. Dogs–War use–United States–Juvenile literature. 2. Human-animal relationships–United States–Juvenile literature. I. Title.
 UH100.G74 2014
 355.4'24–dc23
                                                              2013006740

Text copyright © 2014 by Bellwether Media, Inc. PILOT and associated logos are trademarks and/or registered trademarks of Bellwether Media, Inc. SCHOLASTIC, CHILDREN'S PRESS, and associated logos are trademarks and/or registered trademarks of Scholastic Inc.

Printed in the United States of America, North Mankato, MN.

TABLE OF CONTENTS

A Military Hero 4

To Protect, Sniff, and Search 6

Training for War 12

A Brave Team 14

Outfitted for Danger 16

Retiring from Duty 18

Sergeant Stubby 20

Glossary 22

To Learn More 23

Index 24

A MILITARY HERO

U.S. Army Sergeant Chuck Shuck and his military dog Gabe were on **patrol** with their unit in Iraq. They came to a **suspicious** farmhouse. Chuck gave a command to Gabe. "Seek!" Gabe began to sniff the area. Soon, he located a strange smell inside the farmhouse. He sat down and stared at a pile of clothes. Chuck immediately recognized Gabe's alert. The soldiers investigated and found a box filled with guns hidden beneath the clothes.

But Gabe was not finished. He picked up another strange smell. Gabe led Chuck to a pile of tires outside of the farmhouse. He lay on the ground and stared at the pile. Another alert! Chuck moved a tire. He found 100 rounds of ammunition. The soldiers took the guns and ammunition away. Thanks to Gabe, the enemy could never use these weapons to harm U.S. soldiers.

TO PROTECT, SNIFF, AND SEARCH

Military dogs are important members of armed forces around the world. They provide support on missions and improve **morale** on and off base. In the United States, these canines are officially known as military working dogs, or MWDs. More than 2,500 MWDs serve in the U.S. Armed Forces. Many serve as patrol dogs. They walk with their **handlers** around military bases to guard against **intruders**.

Other military dogs are **deployed** off base with their handlers. Many of them are bomb sniffers. They use their powerful noses to locate deadly homemade bombs called IEDs, or improvised explosive devices. Military dogs also help with dangerous search assignments. The dogs sniff buildings to find illegal drugs. In combat zones, they follow scent trails to locate both enemies and missing soldiers. These brave dogs are often responsible for captures and rescues.

Mission Possible

In 2011, a Belgian Malinois named Cairo helped the U.S. Navy SEALs find wanted terrorist Osama bin Laden.

Dogs have been used for military service since ancient times. The U.S. Army first used dogs during the Revolutionary War. During the Seminole Wars, bloodhounds tracked Native Americans and slaves hiding in Florida swamps. During the Civil War, dogs became messengers and guards.

Civil War

World War II

Vietnam War

War dogs became official helpers during World War II. Many patrolled the U.S. coastlines to guard against the enemy. Other military dogs were sent overseas. There, they guarded soldiers, weapons, and buildings. They carried messages across battlefields and **scouted** enemy locations. Some were trained to attack the enemy on command. War dogs took on a new role in the Vietnam War. They used their keen senses to search Vietnam's thick jungles for enemies and weapons.

Today, the most common military dog breeds are the German Shepherd and Belgian Malinois. Others include the Dutch Shepherd, Labrador Retriever, and Golden Retriever. These breeds possess great strength, courage, and intelligence. They also have extremely sharp senses of smell and hearing.

Breeds of Military Dogs

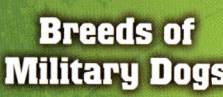
Dutch Shepherd

Labrador Retriever

Golden Retriever

German Shepherd

Profile: Belgian Malinois

Super Sense of Smell
A sensitive nose helps the dog detect drugs and locate injured soldiers on the battlefield.

Fur Coat
A double fur coat lets the dog adapt to all kinds of extreme weather conditions.

Size
Height: 22 to 26 inches (56 to 66 centimeters)

Weight: 50 to 80 pounds (23 to 36 kilograms)

Strong Instincts
The dog has a sharp sense for danger. It keeps itself and other soldiers safe.

The U.S. Navy also uses small dogs, such as terriers and beagles, to search submarines for illegal drugs. These dogs can navigate a sub's narrow spaces with greater ease than large breeds.

TRAINING FOR WAR

Skydiving Dogs
Some military dogs learn to parachute out of airplanes with their handlers.

Most military dogs are trained at Lackland Air Force Base in San Antonio, Texas. Before they begin training, all dogs must pass a physical examination to prove they are healthy and strong. They also have to pass **temperament** tests. Military dogs need to be comfortable around guns and loud noises. They must have a desire to search for objects. The dogs must also be able to act in an aggressive manner.

Dogs that pass these tests enter advanced training. Here, they spend about four months learning special military skills. Most train to be patrol dogs. Others are trained for **detection**. All dogs learn to follow commands both on and off leash. Trainers always use **positive reinforcement** with the dogs. They usually reward dogs with praise. Sometimes they also reward them with toys. Dogs receive **certification** in **obedience** and in their special skill. They must pass tests every year to keep their certification.

A BRAVE TEAM

The dogs are matched with handlers during their training at Lackland. The handlers come from military bases all over the United States. They spend 11 weeks at Lackland training with their dogs. Handlers and dogs learn to communicate with each other. They must be able to recognize each other's signals in an instant. After training at Lackland, they return to their home bases. Now they are ready for a real mission!

Handlers and military dogs spend most of their time together. This helps them form bonds of friendship and trust. They live together. They eat, exercise, and travel as a team. Most dogs sleep in kennels at night. However, some handlers allow their dogs to sleep with them in their beds!

Top Rank

Military dogs are always awarded one rank higher than their handler. This ensures that the dogs are always treated with complete respect.

OUTFITTED FOR DANGER

Military dogs and their handlers are often sent to dangerous combat zones. To stay safe, the dogs wear special gear designed just for them. Dog gas masks protect them from breathing poisonous gas. Dog goggles called "Doggles" protect their eyes from sand and wind. The dogs wear booties to protect their paws from sharp rubble.

Doggles

camera

The dogs also wear special vests to keep them safe. Cooling vests help keep dogs comfortable in hot temperatures. Heavy bulletproof vests called flak jackets protect them in battle. Some vests have cameras and lights. When soldiers send the dogs into buildings or caves, they can see what the dogs see. Often, the vests include speakers so handlers can give their dogs commands. Some vests even have special straps that allow handlers to carry their dogs like a pack.

RETIRING FROM DUTY

Military dogs often **retire** when they are around 10 years old. Most are simply too old to perform their duties. Some retire because of illness or injury. Handlers often adopt their retired military dogs. Law enforcement agencies sometimes adopt younger retired dogs to work as police dogs. Many families also want to adopt retired military dogs. Some wait for years to bring home one of these heroic canines.

MWD Monument
The first national monument to honor military dogs is called the Military Working Dog Teams National Monument. Located at Lackland Air Force Base, the sculpture shows a handler and four military dogs.

Before people adopt a retired military dog, they should be aware that many have special needs. **Post-traumatic stress disorder** (PTSD) is a common problem. In combat, many dogs experienced terrifying situations including gunfire and explosions. These events can affect the dogs for a long time. Even when they are far from combat, the dogs still frighten easily. **Veterinarians** use medicine to treat dogs with PTSD. Loving families help dogs feel safe. In time, most military dogs recover from PTSD and live happy lives.

SERGEANT STUBBY

The United States did not officially allow dogs in the military during World War I. However in 1917, Private John Robert Conroy found a stray dog and kept it. He named the dog Stubby for its short tail. Soon, Stubby became the **mascot** for Conroy's unit. Stubby marched with the soldiers during drills and even learned to salute!

In 1918, Private Conroy **smuggled** Stubby aboard his troop's ship. The ship was headed for France to fight in the war. In France, Stubby became a hero. He warned his unit of enemy attacks and comforted wounded soldiers. Stubby even helped capture an enemy spy. He gripped the man's pants with his teeth.

Stubby served in the war for 18 months and participated in many battles. Although he was hurt several times, he always recovered and returned to duty. The Army gave Stubby the rank of Sergeant for his service to his country. He was the first dog to earn a rank in the U.S. Armed Forces!

GLOSSARY

certification—official recognition that a dog has mastered specific job skills

deployed—brought to a place to begin military action

detection—the identification of something that is hidden

handlers—people who are responsible for highly trained dogs

intruders—people who enter a place without permission

mascot—an animal or person used as a symbol of a group or team

morale—the confidence and enthusiasm of a person or group

obedience—skills that include sit, stay, come, and down

patrol—an assignment or mission

positive reinforcement—using treats, toys, or other rewards to praise good behavior

post-traumatic stress disorder—severe anxiety that occurs after a person experiences a terrifying event

retire—to stop working

scouted—spied or explored to gain information

smuggled—secretly brought something illegal somewhere

suspicious—something that appears to be wrong

temperament—personality or nature

veterinarians—doctors who treat animals

TO LEARN MORE

AT THE LIBRARY

Apte, Sunita. *Combat-Wounded Dogs*. New York, N.Y.: Bearport Pub., 2010.

Goldish, Meish. *War Dogs*. New York, N.Y.: Bearport Pub., 2012.

Ruffin, Frances E. *Military Dogs*. New York, N.Y.: Bearport Pub., 2007.

ON THE WEB

Learning more about military dogs is as easy as 1, 2, 3.

1. Go to www.factsurfer.com.

2. Enter "military dogs" into the search box.

3. Click the "Surf" button and you will see a list of related Web sites.

With factsurfer.com, finding more information is just a click away.

INDEX

adoption, 18, 19
Belgian Malinois, 7, 10, 11
bin Laden, Osama, 7
breeds, 7, 8, 10, 11
certification, 13
Conroy, John Robert, 20
detection, 4, 6, 13
drugs, 6, 11
duties, 6, 8, 9, 13, 20, 21
equipment, 16, 17
France, 20
Gabe, 4, 5
guard, 6, 8, 9
handlers, 6, 12, 14, 15, 16, 17, 18
history, 7, 8, 9, 20, 21
IEDs, 6
Iraq, 4
Lackland Air Force Base, 13, 14, 18

Military Working Dog Teams National Monument, 18
patrol, 4, 6, 9, 13
positive reinforcement, 13
post-traumatic stress disorder, 19
qualities, 10, 11, 13
rank, 15, 21
retirement, 18, 19
senses, 4, 6, 9, 10, 11
Sergeant Stubby, 20, 21
Shuck, Chuck, 4, 5
skills, 6, 12, 13, 20
training, 12, 13, 14
veterinarians, 19

The images in this book are reproduced through the courtesy of: US Department of Defense, front cover, pp. 4, 7, 10, 12, 13, 15, 16, 18; Stacy Pearsall/ Getty Images, front cover; David Livingston/ Getty Images, p. 5; Wicek Listwan Fotografie, p. 10 (top); Foto-ann, p. 10 (middle); Utekhina Anna, p. 10 (bottom); (Collection)/ Prints & Photographs Division/ Library of Congress, pp. 8, 21; Trinity Mirror/ Mirrorpix/ Alamy, p. 9 (left); Everett_Glow/ Glow Images, p. 9 (right); Ysbrand Cosijn, p. 11; Romeo Gacad/ Getty Images, p. 14; US Marines/ Alamy, p. 17; Gregory Bull/ AP Images, p. 19; Bettman/ Corbis/ AP Images, p. 20.

5-15
$14.36

T 577524